SCHOOL REPORT

Student:	Tommy DoLittle	
	FAIL	
Walking	Very lazy boy indeed!	0/10
Running	Doesn't like to run	0/10
Playing	Much too lazy to play	0/10
Reading	Will not read!	0/10
Jumping	Cannot jump at all	0/10
Sleeping	His best subject!	10/10
Dozing	Top marks for Tommy!	10/10
Snoring	Top of the class	10/10
Resting	Works hard at it	10/10

Tommy DoLittle is a very lazy boy.

He doesn't like to do anything at all-- except sleep!

Headmaster   *John Rowe*

Mr. J. A. Rowe

Humdrum School for Boys

Copyright © 2002 by Michael Neugebauer Verlag, an imprint of Nord-Süd Verlag AG, Gossau Zürich, Switzerland
First published in Switzerland under the title *Tommy DoLittle*.

First published in the United States, Great Britain, Canada,
Australia, and New Zealand in 2002 by North-South Books,
an imprint of Nord-Süd Verlag AG, Gossau Zürich, Switzerland.

Distributed in the United States by North-South Books Inc., New York.

Library of Congress Cataloging-in-Publication Data is available.
A CIP catalogue record for this book is available from The British Library.
ISBN 0-7358-1718-9 (trade edition) 10 9 8 7 6 5 4 3 2 1
ISBN 0-7358-1719-7 (library edition) 10 9 8 7 6 5 4 3 2 1
Printed in Italy

For more information about our books, and the authors and artists
who create them, visit our web site: www.northsouth.com

A Michael Neugebauer Book · North-South Books · New York / London

I must not sleep in class
I must not sleep in class
I must not sleep in class
I must not sleep in class
I must not sleep in class
I must not sleep in class
I must not sleep in class
I must not sleep in class
I must not sleep in
I must not sleep
I must sleep in
I must sleep
I sleep
sleep

Tommy DoLittle

by John Rowe

This is the tale of Tommy DoLittle, the laziest boy in the world.

He was so lazy, his dog had to take *him* for walks!

One day, while Tommy was hiding behind a book to avoid being called on by his teacher, a strange and mysterious thing happened. Before Tommy DoLittle knew what he was doing, he began to actually *look* at the book.

Words danced across the pages, bright pictures dazzled him.
He just *had* to take a closer look. . . .

Suddenly, words and pictures began to spin through the air with *a swish!*

Tommy DoLittle squeezed his eyes shut and called for his mother, "HELP!" But his cries were swept away in a sparkling whirlwind.

Nobody could help him now. He was being dragged deeper into the story.

When Tommy DoLittle dared to open his eyes again,
he let out a shriek of terror.
"Oh, no! I've turned black and white!"

Before he could catch his breath, the story carried Tommy DoLittle off again. . . .

"*Now* I'm upside down in Australia!" moaned Tommy DoLittle.

"Why, just look at all these funny creatures!"

"Uh oh, I'm falling off Australia! If I tear my pyjamas my mother will be really mad."

"Oh, dear, SNAKES! I'd better get out of here!"

*Before you continue,
read this secret message.
Are you a scaredy-cat?
If so, do NOT turn the page!
If not,
follow Tommy if you dare!

*To read the secret message, just look into the magic mirror.

"Hmmm. . . I wonder what's behind this door. I'll just sneak a peek."

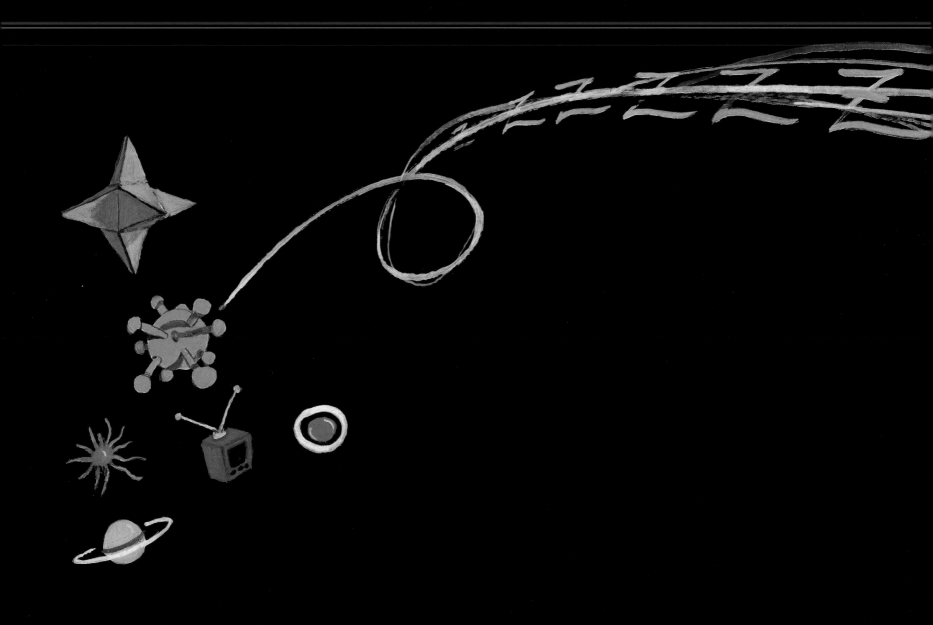

"I don't think my mother will like it at all if I'm abducted by aliens!"

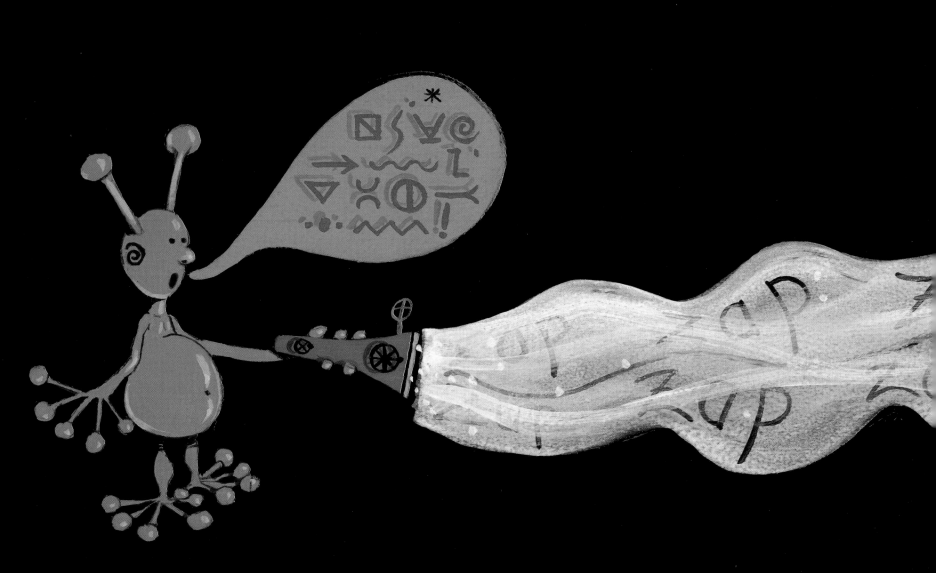

* Take me to your leader...!

"Tommy DoLittle, you naughty boy! Just look at your new pyjamas! How did you manage to get so dirty when all you do is sit around all day?"

"But . . ."